Little and the Buffalo

Story by Jenny Giles
Illustrations by Rachel Tonkin

Rigby
A Harcourt Achieve Imprint

www.Rigby.com
1-800-531-5015

Little Chimp was playing
in the tall grass
by the river.

Big Chimp was down
by the river, too.

4

Little Chimp
saw a buffalo.
"Oo! Oo! Oo!"
said Little Chimp.
"I don't want that buffalo
to get me!"
So he climbed a tree.

The buffalo went down
to the river.

"**Oo**!" said Little Chimp.

"I don't want the buffalo
to get Big Chimp!"

So Little Chimp called out,

"Big Chimp!

Here comes a buffalo!"

But Big Chimp

did not look up.

Little Chimp called out again,

and this time

Big Chimp looked around.

The buffalo
looked around, too.
He saw Little Chimp
up in the tree.

The buffalo ran at the tree
and hit it with his head.
The tree moved!
"Oo!　Oo!　Oo!"
said Little Chimp.

Big Chimp came running
up from the river.

Big Chimp climbed
into a bigger tree
and shouted at the buffalo.
The buffalo ran
at the big tree
and hit it with his head.

But the big tree
did not move.

Little Chimp climbed over
to the big tree.

14

Then the two chimps
jumped up and down
and shouted at the buffalo.

The buffalo stopped
hitting the tree
and went away.
Little Chimp was **very** happy.